GARLANDS OF DARK WATER

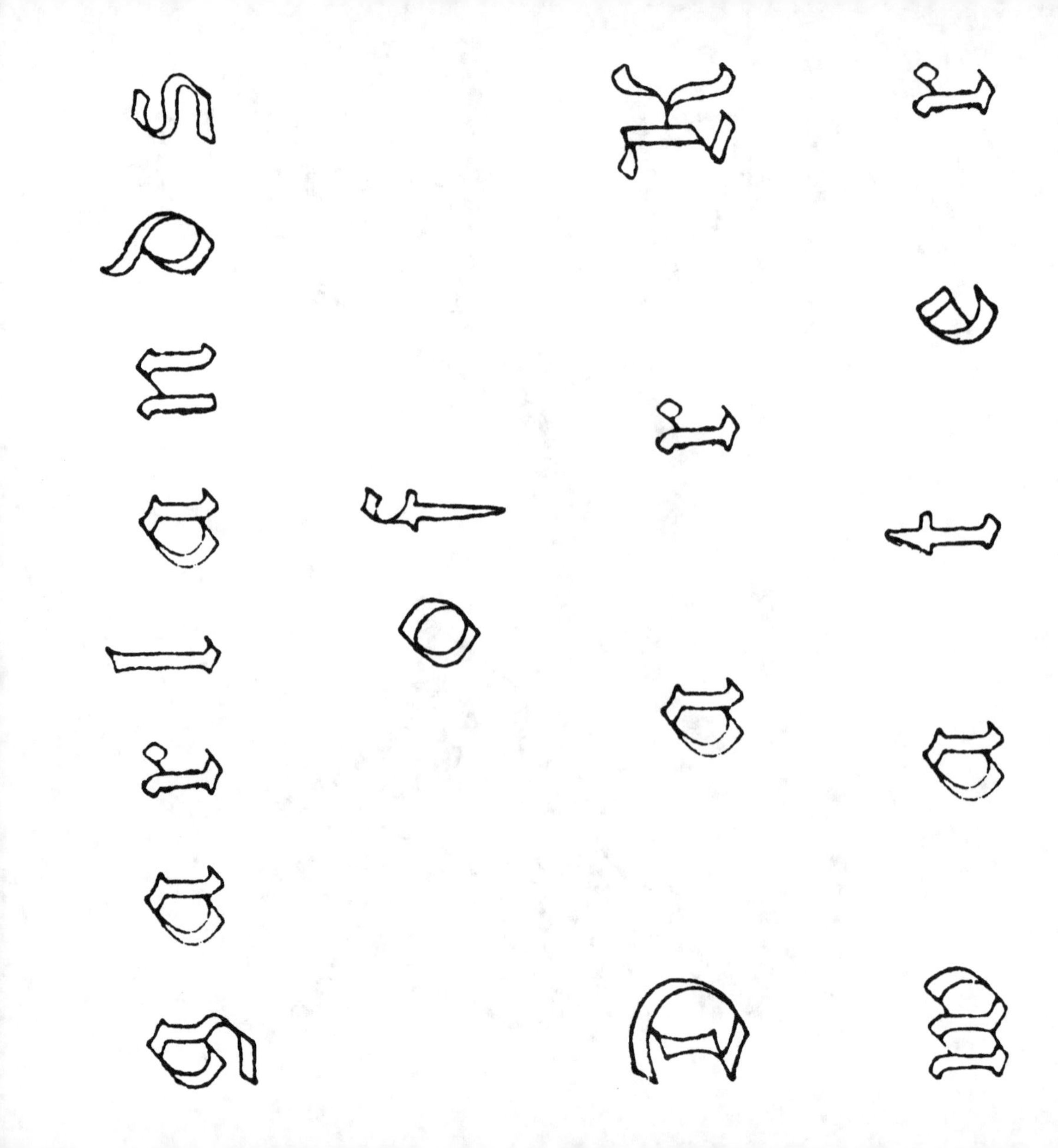

written by
Maggie von Sacher

feral Dove
Bangor, Maine
2024

Welcome...

flip the page

to

enter.

 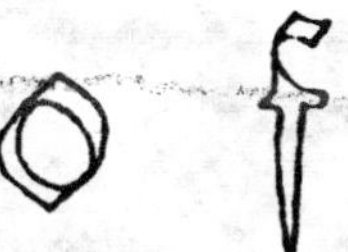 

is not ensured by victory

I care most about feeling expensive,
as if held in stirrups

Extinction blinks and I am
indeterminately staring

A beam of light
chars the sea inside of me

One should keep a lens
on the cold meat of the world

I had my turn of weakness,
her great lie-lined spoon

I had to get it together
Cash in my higher affairs

*Heaping trash inside
the wasteland of my mother*

*My basest fantasy is of the womb's
heat-warped rubble*

*I have little patience
for the medium of news,*

like dried blood on a cleat

*Tragically,
love is presumed of mothers*

*Tragically,
love is presumed of mothers*

*Tragically,
love is presumed of mothers*

like a tractor

I loved to be fawned over
by out-of-town men

I would spend money I didn't have
on earrings the size of keys

S w a l l o w e d

Daughter, oyster,

flicker,

heart

heat

an   anima

to the self,

that some inedible
color is created
Bringing the crayon to my lips

I touch the
heat behind the window

The paper glows
almost beseechingly

She is vivid to look at through
firedancing

Made of death, loved to death

That when I lay down, it's to feed
a hell that has no earth

If I swear to be more awake,
I know especially what I can't
privately do

I take a self-denying
bite down on the wax

It takes one by surprise to be
thought of as beautiful

To be hot enough to forge,
but too hot to touch

Like

a

m o u s e

I cower

in

the

light

Naked as a mirror

and my covered heart
smacking

Bags and Bags and Bags of clothes

the

n   i   g   h   t

was a ring

of gin and grapefruit

The lilacs were sordidly
half-eaten

I fear our sleep is a debt to the law

That love won't manifest

and that we made the law godly
because we lived by it

I want something
much more contentious than
a buzz

To blow air through
the skill between us

To wean my lips on
the craving for the rest

So drunk was all that ensued

In every timeline, I was interviewed

by a whiskey-gold noose

Its shining rope in the air

We vacationed in our back yard,
verdant snores coming from our stables

I was entered
through violet wrists

I looked from waterbound eyes
at the dark specimens of blood before me

Love is how I know I have skin
in the game

Making it up as we go, though
the events feel curated to our tastes:

getting caught, doing the time

was all that ensued

what are the voracious ants doing

to the soft-cooked ground

A life the years aimed at
cheapening by the mouthful

Lower and lower into the crumbs

Until I came down like an acre of land

I invented this kind of groveling

Wound-like tongue, staked
down in the thaw

I imagined the soul of our bed settling
Like water in my shoes

There was a
stretch of land I loved,

Nights were dealt asking for
the phone, and the dark

was packed like firewood

Sometimes, I thought I was shy,
a birdsome man

I punched in and out accordingly
But really, I was an addict

Bettered by the ways liquor
made my pain apparent

Our feral cabinet will
one day be like a church dress

just a specter of suffering…
engulfed, a fear of the thing

My anger has no complaint to wage
of the blousey beauty

Can we get out of here?
I say it with amateur realness

I smoke the page and
Do more than imagine

to talK naKedly of

I feel the pity oggling
in my heart

for the next-best-thing,
on sale

I bring my hand to my breast
A plethora of wetness on my plate

My hand like a torch that fell,
leaving tracks in the snow

An oracle that could sense
through the garden

into the nectar
into the snow of a knife

Petals stop her drain,
like from the reddest cut

Like the world, she was made of time

The knee is our favorite stain,
as it swells behind the solidity

of a white dress

She pulls at my hand,
though my hand

makes a show of refusing

As if to say with a chord:
"Do me this one key kindness"

I mull the old scent,
which is like quicksand

Quicksand against wallpaper

I want to believe there's nothing to fear
about family, yet everything finds

the rotten bitch in my heart

She is dressed and made up

life a town

the train used to run through,
not entirely scabbed over

The feeding on the artist,
and then to lay around
with carpet for eyes

Our mouths propped open
All carbon black and
wanting as much junk as there is
continent

What's going on with the
girl behind the phone?
The flies in the next room over

Paradisic, paradisic,
parasitic

The side of me that is light, the half
of me that is mind-made-up

Whether we're old or new,
it comes easy
And, a life of modesty -
I would never think to marry the two again

My head will do to finds its warm seat,
What a lark will do just
just to get to the inside of a neck

Blood and milky mud

each light touched

s   c   a   l   e

of sunset was esphyxiated

Why am I afraid to feel my breast?

Is that where I become my Mother
Having her cancer, having her prayers
of unbelief

Having her synergistic evil,
and petting where her things sleep

Taking notice of godliness
and where it is stored

Starchasing from a truckbed

At the center of her decorum,
even a spill has its right timing

Pollution bends like the shape
of a flock through the night

and it bleeds from the Hers & Hers towels

Passerby I was to my

own change of heart, like a flash
From the densest ache to praise

The engine revs
Enthralled then dies!

Her stacks of lifeless albums
Mine is the arc
of the inflated paramour,
wrapped in talons and lost to history

We are opposites but
see each other the same

That is my inverted prize
That is the hitch around my neck

Everything cuts me open like asphalt
Afterall, a parking lot was my heart's seat

Don't condemn me to

a house I can't hear at night

Perhaps there is a root evil
where my conscience used to
interest me

I sat window-side, with the
carnage of my mouth out

The tv turns me on
I feel just the crawling of the engine,
like cotton candy skies on my skin

I give the
thought of you a life

Our loyalties were once as old man
and muse -- that is to say, much the
other way around

and it was lovely
to be opinioned and
to be painted on

To hold the sweat out
like a child, its eyes
higher gone
and higher gone
l
To force a blind
worm out of the underground
from the anus
at the top of me

i touch the paintings in the gallery with

Hoping to be an indiscretion, a spot
Of something beautiful
I have always
wanted attention
for how I bore my half of it
Wanted corporate representation,
so I could cease my searching
As newsworthy as a
barnyard kitty
But the way it made me inquire
into my sitting beliefs…
I felt like gin down a bottle
I am akin to
something bitter or worse, since I
Could never see
sweetness as cunning
People forget about the
those of us here,
split down the spine by the world
Through the silken dial tones
of mosquitos

And if I am not overly careful,
I might fall into a penchant
for boys who live on dregs
My hair, sweatered in mud
My strewn brunette winds
That's why I fell open
It pushed the sharpness of bone in,
like a spring rain
And my voice like a cunt
against the spring air
I effort it
It was for the love of the pursuit
I nothing but ran away from my country
The ground will accept a body into its
trickle of curved and versatile fingers
Does the body suck
the ground?
Past the sodomy and
into the exquisite custard
And all in the span of what seemed like
one dwindling, week of nights

full vanity

She gave me a

Key

to a

sauna   liKe

r   o   o   m

I passed through
the key, like a mouth to a hose
The warmth
having disabled my microchip
This quality, of always
turning, was the hypothermic
race to her heart
The cursor between
here and the mothership
I felt the pinch of the leash:
my every dim-faced calorie
extinguished
for a piece of her prurient desire, like an oyster bed
The more I pulled, the faster her favor grew
Like the sinew of a dollar bill

i

slurred

my

surprise.

errant ocean waves
Gorgeous men in the
August heat
The nights pressed ahead,
the edge of the known world
like lapis
I thought the
unthinking bug-like dark
was handsome

Two become one cooling sweetness
My tongue lain with sticky heat
and dreamless sleep
The dirt of being singleminded
was all over me,
a scar layer of plaque
August dealt in curious things,
in feelings that were misheard

in the day
Sheer, purple
Wireless and intermittent
I don't have the imprint
of being from somewhere
Maybe I'm from the ceiling
Something regal about
a torn swing,
A tickling in the fruit like a worm
My home is run by kitsch
The more nevermore, the
Wormier the fruit's aberration

Down

Made to fall down
Body, like a finger
We take the
cursed living on our backs
Like atomized freckles
Like lone curls
on the watered sand
Waitressing our way
from left hand to right hand

The love with which we attempt
these mornings
is tired and unclued about the time
The gas station overhang imposes
on the lunch of sky
We go back
and forth - a twenty, a fifty -
Followed by the hallway
Changed by the need
to cut the stink of the tree down

Doing the time
I let my hair hang,
like loose cigar smoke
Meat sliced by a knife,
patently purple at its core
My finger like the trigger of a drill

Walking the smoothed out path,
the fire-colored conceits
of the ground
I would not shed
this insipid taste of normalcy
The world but without its gall
It is in admitting my insignficance
that I seal my fate

Why should Earth have
to make secret progress?
Her glare is like sediment in my glass
My hangover's halo,
endeavoring to be taken out like trash
A passion to
protect the future,
but from what responsibilities?
I am an assassin of the future
Loving her gives me
jet lag
A grape world to debut,
but gun-shy
My head like cool metal too

getting

caught

i

fell

out

with

I fell out with a friend
Arms out with dinner plates like a
found sense of metal
The cars look like they are looking
There they are but I am
a thousand aims and reasons faster
I sweep aside your bangs
I love it fast and local, down to the bite
Down to the
the blind-white signature line
I love it when we turn the control button
on each other, and the failing questions
burn us whole
The toes fall off in orderly lops
Eventually the foot is shorn and clear as the
vinyl is yawning, yawning
Love wants to be
star-shaped skin

All wheeling creation, the thingy
flesh of a borderhole
Now I have a file with my name on it
Now I have a love whom every hire can cross
A love that wants to be crude, more
undescribed than something made of work
The kitchen shook
Was it calling its transmission
to my mind? the speed
at which they took me
More than the surface can say,
not even a pan left out where
my side is
From evenings of corn to bloody fingers,
there is no discordance except love here
We appear to be dressing a tight little pass
Our punches land on wood-scrape
She and I watch
as a southerly, white storm is thrust

fingers

fingers.

i can't

distinguish
Mother, like an apple
on a flood
The smell of kerosene
linked my crazy to hers
Our breath jumped
like a dog's
We were raising
ourselves from revelation
to fetish
Desire directed me
to the floor of the car
I care, I queer
The contingency I didnt arrange for
was being as victim
as I was young

EPI
LOGUE

Your
first look
burned
beyond me
At my back,
the feel of cash
My debts were
sapphic
Only women or
death would
avenge me
The long gait
of the
mornings like
being smothered
by muscle, or
being slid into by
oleander cartridges

I never mentioned
how cumbersomely I
felt the
piling on of
each buzz,
couched in my
mounting and
mounting want:
my pet amygdala
Didn't let on
how I was
corrupted by
a lack of money
Afraid to turn
around, sure
to be found out
I liked the
cold physics of society,
and my learned

place in it
I tried
scissoring through
life conversationally,
vapidly
A soundless
buffer
always ashed
between me and
progress
So I was not
a thinker of regard
But when the
news of you
came, I walked
your outline
with my mind
You were mud-stuck
in me

The embattled hunger
of pregnancy
Oil wars were
as much as I could see
Where the reaches
of the eye
horizon,
I found a gift
that estranged
me from others
It was a rebirth into
selfishness
that fertilized my egg
The earth lay in
a plague of cold
that was root deep,
but I wanted to
lie with you and

Warmth that could
shiver up the
thin walls
Finally, my recovery
was boded, and
I was jealous to pay
for a look at
it
This was no
stoned joyride
of pretend
Windows cracked,
harvest air pulsing in
I had never done
anything
with life-bearing
in mind
The backend of a breath
that took a year, the rearview
in the mirror
Anyway, how different
Is it really
The viscous
blue glare
of birth or of the tv
I trap the
pending soon in my hand
Like bloodshot
round cherries
The soft C of
"recessed" belly
This kind
Of love, I know

I will never
live it down

The enD.

ACKNOWLEDGMENTS

I must thank God for always meeting me with unconditional love, for asking nothing of me and yet giving me so much to celebrate. This book is comprised of poems that were written during the ongoing COVID pandemic. As such, I would like to thank the medical and care workers and disability activists, who carry the weight of a system that brutally fails so many. Likewise, I am thinking of the Palestinian hospital workers in Gaza, to whose example we owe everything, everything.

Maggie Von Sacher (she/her) is a communist
and writer based all over the South, her work
is concerned with the enjoyment of the gothic.

IG: @godsufferstoo

Substack: godsufferstoo.substack.com

THANK YOU FOR BEING HERE

FERAL DOVE

COVER & INTERIOR BOOK DESIGN

BY EVAN FEMINO

feraldove.com

PUBLISHED BY FERAL DOVE BOOKS

ISBN 979-8-9856764-6-4